Coffee break stories

Five short stories from a crime thriller writer

Stephen W Follows

Stephen W Follows

Published August 2010 by Stephen W Follows

Authors note

Although some actual locations and titles are used, these stories are
works of fiction.
Any resemblance to actual events, organisations, or persons,
living or dead, is entirely coincidental.

ISBN 978-0-9566109-1-1

Published by Stephen W Follows
Jericho Road
Newark
NG24 3GT

Printed by CPI Anthony Rowe
Bumpers Farm, Chippenham

Stephenwfollows.co.uk

The stories
(Reading times in brackets)

Story number one

Mr Morecambe's favourite pen

Tragedy comes to a family with a haunted history

'Mummy? What's a polzergiest?'

'Poltergeist, sweetheart; it's like a ghost that no one can see.'

'If you can't see them, why does Daddy work with them?'

Jane Morecambe took a deep breath. 'I don't think Daddy does work with them, Jessica; why would he work with a ghost?'

'Because when Uncle David was here talking to Daddy yesterday he said that it was the poltergeist that Daddy was having trouble with at work and that it was the poltergeist that kept moving Daddy's pen on his desk.'

'Oh, I see,' replied Jane. 'Well you had better ask Daddy then when he gets in from work. Chocolate brownies will be ready soon.'

'Yippee!'

Two hours later Mike Morecambe arrived home from work. Jessica was almost ready for bed and he took her upstairs for one more of her favourite bed-time stories.

After her four chocolate brownies and a glass of milk, Jessica was soon fast asleep and Mike – like a million other husbands that night - joined his wife in front of the television with a glass of wine.

'She didn't ask you about Poltergeists did she?' said Jane.

'No, why?'

'Apparently she heard you and David talking yesterday about work. Something about your pen being moved?'

'Oh crikey, yes. I was just telling David that my favourite pen, you know the old fountain pen? It had gone missing a few times and had turned up on someone else's desk.'

Jane moved in her chair, preparing for Coronation Street, and rolled her eyes. 'I don't know why you don't get a new one anyway, it's ancient, I'm surprised you can still buy the ink for it.'

Mike, slightly hurt, replied, 'It was good enough for my Grandad, it's good enough for me.'

After a few minutes silence, Jane's gaze left the television. She looked at her husband. He was falling asleep. She was going to let him, but he stirred as though he sensed her looking.

'Don't forget I'm going to Linda's tomorrow night,' she said. 'Jessica's staying with Amy and her mum and dad down the road.'

'Yes, okay, I'll be working until about nine; I'll get a takeaway. How is my sister anyway? Still banging on about the past?'

'It's called genealogy! Don't be so miserable, it's interesting.'

Mike nodded his head in a condescending way and changed the subject. 'And you haven't forgotten have you that I'm doing the night shift this Saturday?'

'I had forgotten yes,' said Jane. 'Oh well, I'll ask Jessica if she wants to have her friend to stay. And I think

2

your big sister said she might pop round for a glass of wine next time I was on my own.'

John Handbury was tired as he approached the gates on Saturday morning. The sign he looked at every morning was old and shabby, but it still made him get out of bed every day.   GERALD   HANDBURY   &   SON. GENERAL HAULIERS.

He had meant to change the sign for some time now and use more modern ideas like LOGISTICS or FREIGHT SPECIALISTS but his customers were loyal and he didn't think a new name would change anything. Besides, he thought, what would his Great Grandad, the founder, make of it.

The gate man waved him through politely, but John only noticed him subconsciously as he raised his hand in acknowledgment and made his way to his parking bay.

The first delivery made by Gerald Handbury in 1894 was 78 cartons of eggs by horse and cart. John Handbury's parking bay was on exactly the same spot that Gerald had loaded up his first consignment. A plaque reminded every visitor as they approached reception. The current modern building was a thousand times bigger than the original sheds and the only other reminder of the past was John's desk, hopelessly out of place in the modern office. it had been built for his grandfather, Gerald's son, when he took over the company. It was oak, huge, scarred, and over-polished.

'Bye! Got to go!' Shouted Mike Morecambe as he opened his front door. Jane was upstairs washing her hair and Jessica wouldn't have noticed if there was fire and smoke coming from the settee; Chuckle Vision was on.

Travelling to work on a Saturday was much easier and he arrived ten minutes early at 17.50 for the night shift. He had worked for Gerald Handbury & Son for 15 years and had got to know John Handbury and other board members very well.

Mike had worked his way up to be Senior Transport Manager, and when certain people didn't come up with the goods, it was Mike who would jump in and sort things out; as he was doing this particular Saturday night.

As he was climbing the stairs to his second floor office that looked out over the warehouse, he came across John Handbury.

'Hello Mike,' said Handbury in his friendly way. 'You're the one looking after things tonight eh?'

Mike smiled back as he replied. 'Well, you know what they say; if you want a good job doing, do it your...'

'Yeah, yeah I know, is this where you ask for more money?'

'Wouldn't dream of it, sir.'

Then Handbury paused as though he had thought of something else. 'Where are you working from tonight then?' he said.

'Well, my office, unless you're sacking me!'

'No one told you then, obviously,' said Handbury. 'Your office is being decorated over the weekend with some others on the second floor.'

'Ah, right,' said Mike thoughtfully. 'Oh well, looks like a desk in the warehouse then.'

Handbury raised his hand and pointed a finger in the air. 'Don't be daft, Mike, you can use my office.'

'No, John, really, it's not necessary.'

'Of course it is, you can still see down into the warehouse from there, come on, I insist. You can use my computer, it will access everything that yours can; password is Lucy1234; our pet dog's name by the way.'

Three minutes later, Mike was looking out of the window of John Hanbury's office. He could see most of the warehouse and the despatch area. He retrieved what papers he needed from his own office and settled down at John Handbury's desk to do his work.

It was approaching 1 a.m. when Kevin Bolland, Shift Foreman, reported to Mike on the despatch schedule. 'Only one to go now, Mike.'

'Good stuff, Kev, which one?'

'That load of kitchen rolls to the Johnson's distribution centre in Broxburn, Big Arthur said he would take it; okay with you?'

'Sure, after this I think Arthur's on holiday anyway, so we won't need to worry about his hours.'

Kevin gave the thumbs up and turned to get back to work. Then Mike remembered his duties. 'Hey, Kev; you know what Johnson's are like with their quality control and ISO 9001. This will be the first time we've used their new despatch note. The original will have to be signed by me remember, by hand.'

'Okay, I'll bring everything up just before Arthur's ready to go.

Mike looked at the clock in John Handbury's office. Something else that didn't fit the modern decor. It's huge brown casing shone like the glass that protected it and the words *Abbey Of Lincoln* stood out behind the hands like a proud boast. He remembered being asked once to lend a hand to get it down for cleaning and how John had nearly had a heart attack when they almost dropped it.

The time was 1.55 a.m. and he knew Kevin would be back soon for the final signature on the new despatch

5

note. He took his pen from shirt pocket. He had never been exactly sure of its history but he knew it was given to his father by his grandfather many years ago. Some of his work colleagues would joke about the 'old Bic' and he had been disappointed of late when it had gone missing only to turn up on someone else's desk.

It was, in fact, a Mereberger, made in Switzerland, with fine gold leaf patterns on a dark brown porcelain casing. He had read on a website that not many of them had been made and that one had been used by Stanley Baldwin when he was Chancellor of the Exchequer in 1922. They were also becoming quite rare and he estimated the value at £750. But the value meant nothing to him. When his father died, Mike had continued to use it and had become accustomed to it. He reached for the bottle of ink he kept in his briefcase and carefully replenished the pen, while he waited for Kevin.

Twenty minutes later, Kevin arrived with the documents and put them down in front of Mike. 'There we are then, Mike, just three signatures please, and print and date.'

Mike signed the three papers Kevin had laid out for him. They both went down into the warehouse to see Big Arthur off. Mike was pleased to see Arthur cleaning his lights and his windows. He let Arthur finish his cleaning and went over to him. 'Take care, Arthur, the surfaces look slippy.'

'Always do, Mike,' said Arthur. 'At least I'll have good light; it's a full moon.'

'Ooh, be careful then, Arthur,' said Kevin jokingly. 'You know what they say about strange happenings when there's a full moon!'

Mike and Kevin watched the lorry move slowly out of the gates and listened to its throaty engine until there was silence. Kevin turned to Mike as he took off his woolen gloves. 'I'll get going then Mike if you don't mind, no point hanging around now all the works been done.'

'Sure, get yourself home, Kevin, I'll lock up. I won't be far behind you.'

Mike made his way to John Handbury's office to collect his belongings and leave things as he had found them. As he walked into the office he noticed that the light had been switched off. Looking back, he saw that all the corridor lights were still switched on. I didn't switch this light off, he thought to himself. Kevin? No, he left the office before I did and got straight into his car to go home when I was still downstairs. Who else then? Night staff? No, he was the last. Security? Not on a Saturday. I.T. staff? No. Cleaners? No. He decided to shout around. 'Hello! Mike Morecambe here! Anyone else left in the building?'

Nothing.

He switched on the light in the office and made his way to the desk. His pen was missing. 'Someone's playing silly fools again,' he said out loud to himself. Then he noticed a blank piece of paper on the desk with one word written on it. As he moved around the front of the desk, he realised that the word had been written with his missing pen. Just one word; underlined – MURDERERS!

He looked around quickly as though he might be surrounded by intruders, but soon realised again, he was alone. He made sure his pen was nowhere else in the room and picked up the sheet of paper from the desk and put it into his pocket. On his way outside he took the long route around the departments to check that he was indeed alone.

He was.

As he pulled up in his car to lock the gates behind him, he noticed the full moon and remembered what Kevin had said jokingly to Big Arthur.

He awoke at 11.55 on Sunday morning. Jane was in the bedroom hanging new curtains and she turned to speak to him when she realised he was awake. 'Morning, darling, didn't here you get in this morning, what time was it?'

'About three.'

'Oh not too late then, well you can relax and have your brunch; Jessica has gone to play next door.'

Mike pulled his dressing gown over himself and made his way to the en-suite for his ritual of covering his face with cold water. Jane gave a satisfying 'There' as she stood back to see her handy work.

'Did you see Linda last night?' said Mike.

'Yes, she popped round for an hour to keep me company.'

'And how is my big sister?'

'She's fine,' replied Jane. 'By the way, you know she's doing this family genealogy?'

'Mm,' said Mike in an uninterested way.

'Well, your great grandfather was born just a few miles away, did you realise?'

'No I didn't.'

Mike decided he would not mention the note that someone had left in John Handbury's office. When Jane left the room he took it from the drawer that he had put it in a few hours earlier. As he looked at it again, he could not decide if he should laugh it off or take it seriously and let someone know.

After a few minutes they were both together again in the kitchen. Mike sipped his coffee as Jane revisited the genealogy. 'Well?' she said.

'Well what?'

'Don't you want to know where your great grandfather was born?'

'Oh yes, you said a few miles away.'

Jane seemed to hesitate as she answered. 'Munckton.'

'Munckton eh,' said Mike. 'All that family history and all within four miles of here.'

Jane did not offer any more information, which was unusual for her, so Mike prompted her. 'Anything else about him? What did he do for a living?'

'Oh he was a farrier,' said Jane.

'A good honest trade, what's wrong with that?' asked Mike.

'Nothing.'

'So why did you say it with hesitation?'

Jane put down her cup. 'Well there's something else,' she said. 'Awful really.'

'Trust my big sister,' said Mike. 'What's she found out then?'

'Your great grandfather was executed 1897.'

Mike paused for a while before he reacted. 'Bloody hell, that's just why I didn't want to get into this genealogy, I told Sis she would find out things we didn't want to know, I just knew it.'

'Anyway it was a long time ago,' said Jane, trying to calm him.

'Suppose so,' replied Mike. 'What was he executed for anyway?'

'Murder. He stabbed someone in the neck.'

'Bloody hell Jane! Are you telling me I'm a descendent of someone that went round knifing people?'

Jane waited before answering. 'He didn't use a knife.'

'What?'

'He used a pen.'

Mike dropped his coffee cup and it shattered on the floor.

John Handbury arrived at work as usual on the Monday morning. He was pleased to see that the weekend decorators had finished their work and that Mike had put things back in place in his office. Mike would.

The duty foreman reminded him that Mike would be starting later because of his Saturday night shift. He checked the delivery schedules for the foreman and instructed him accordingly. Mrs. Childs knocked on his door and walked in slowly. She had been the head cleaner at the company for 17 years and she knew exactly when to bring John Handbury his tea before she left. She placed the cup and saucer in front of him and after the usual morning exchanges she reached into her pocket. 'And by the way, Mr. Handbury, I kept this safe for you, you must have dropped it.'

She handed him Mike Morecambe's pen.

'It was by the leg of your desk, sort of inside it, so you wouldn't have seen it easily.'

'Thank you, Mrs. Childs; but it's not mine.'

'Well anyway, I'll be off,' she answered, as though it must have been and he didn't know what he was talking about. Handbury smiled as she left, because he knew what she was thinking.

He looked at the pen and put it to the front of his desk. He seemed to remember that Mike Morecambe had a pen that was dear to him and he surmised that Mike had dropped it when he was using the office.

Jane Morecambe had arrived back home after taking Jessica to school that same morning. Mike came downstairs as he was straightening his tie to find her reading something at the dining room table.

She looked up to acknowledge him. 'Morning, what time are you starting today then?'

10

'Oh I don't need to be there until about eleven after my Saturday night shift. What's that you're reading?'

'It's a copy of a newspaper clipping about your great grandfather; just confirms what I told you yesterday really. How do you feel about it now after a night's sleep?'

'Okay, can I have a look?'

Jane passed him the paper. It was a copy of a short article in the Daily Express, March 10th 1897.

'Herbert Angelo Morecambe was hanged yesterday in the downstairs gallows room at Birmingham prison. Morecambe was found guilty last month of murdering his victim by stabbing him in the neck with a pen. Lord Justice Rowan, in sentencing Morecambe, had said that disputes over pay and conditions did not give the defendant the right to take it on himself to stab his employer and that he was clearly a danger to society with his unstable disposition.

Morecambe stabbed his employer, Gerald Handbury, in his office following an argument over pay and working conditions at the stables where Handbury kept horses for his hauliers business and where Morecambe was employed as a farrier…'.

Mike put the paper down and looked at Jane. 'I don't suppose my big sister could be wrong about all of this could she?'

'No, she said she checked it all loads of times and all the stories and cuttings tie in with each other.'

Mike sat down, sighed and put his head in his hands. 'So let me get this straight; my great grandfather stabbed Gerald Handbury, the founder of Handbury and Son, who I now work for, in the neck, with a pen. Gerald Handbury died and my great grandfather was hanged for murder.'

'That's about it,' replied Jane.

Two hours later, Mike arrived at work. He decided to go straight up and see John Handbury. He related the whole story to Handbury who did not move in his chair as he listened intently. When Mike had finished, Handbury told him to sit down. He leaned forward and handed the pen that Mrs. Childs had found over to him. 'This is yours I take it?'

'Yes, where did you find it?'

'Mrs. Childs found it under the desk.'

Because Handbury did not respond to the story, Mike continued. 'So what do you make of it then?'

'Not sure what to think, Mike. I had heard some tales from my father, but I probably just brushed it all off. He used to talk about some ghost or poltergeist thing that was the ghost of Gerald Handbury.'

'There's something else, John; this pen that Mrs. Childs found, it was used to write this that I found on your desk last night after I had been down in the warehouse.'

Mike took the piece of paper that said *Murderers* on it from his pocket and passed it to Handbury. After briefly taking it in, Handbury looked up at Mike. 'We need to tell the police, Mike, don't you think?'

'Not sure what they could do.'

'Maybe find out who wrote this?'

Handbury's office door suddenly slammed shut with a tremendous noise. Both men jumped and looked at the door with amazement. No one else was in the area. The two men looked at each other. Then the handle on the door was turning again. Handbury went over to the door, grabbed the handle and flung the door open as fast as he could, hoping to catch someone on the other side. No one was there.

12

One hour later, Detective Constable Manors turned up at reception. Handbury had told the receptionist to expect someone. 'Will you go up please,' she said. 'They're both waiting for you, second floor, first office on the left.'

'Thank you,' said Manors as he made his way towards the stairs. He found the door that said John Handbury on it and knocked twice. No answer. He knocked again. No answer. He opened the door and walked in as he said, 'hello? D.C. Manors.'

What he saw was enough to make him freeze where he stood.

Mike Morecambe was on the floor, face down. Blood was covering the floor around his head. His own Mereberger pen had been rammed into his neck. Handbury was standing by his desk looking down at Mike, shivering.

Manors shouted at Handbury. 'Stay where you are! Don't move!'

Handbury shook his head. 'It wasn't me!'

Manors grabbed Handbury, spun him round and cuffed him. Handbury shouted again. 'It wasn't me! I just turned to look out of the window and when I turned back he was falling to the floor holding his neck!'

Manors bent down over Mike Morecambe and put two fingers on the side of his neck. He reached for the phone. 'DC Manors, get an ambulance down to Handbury Hauliers, and a SOCO squad. And err, tell the ambulance not to hurry.'

Handbury persisted. 'It was not me; it must have been the poltergeist!'

'What?' said Manors with an air of sympathy.

'The poltergeist, the ghost of my great grandfather. My great grandfather was killed by his great grandfather. It's revenge don't you see! Revenge.'

Four weeks later Jane Morecambe was making chocolate brownies again for Jessica. She stopped for a while to wipe the tears from her eyes as Jessica came into the kitchen with her friend.

'Mummy, I have told Isabelle about daddy, but she doesn't understand, she says he must be somewhere.'

Jane nodded and smiled. She went to the back door to take out the full bin liner and the newspapers. One of the newspapers fell from her hands and she noticed an article as she picked it up.

'John Handbury, owner of Handbury and Son Hauliers was jailed for 22 years yesterday for the murder of one of his employees. He had pleaded not guilty and had said that a poltergeist was responsible'.

Jane threw everything into the bin and slammed the lid shut in anger. As she walked back, the back door closed. She opened it and called out to Jessica. 'Why did you close the door Jessica?'

'I didn't Mummy; I'm playing in here.'

In at the deep end

A young journalist learns the hard way

Tuesday 07.35

The sign above the main doors said 'News with a difference'. Matt Melbourne hesitated for a while to read it again. Right, he thought, I need to do something different and unusual to make my mark.

The next sign he noticed was on the editor's door as he knocked on it.

Diane Mathers
Editor
If it does not excite you
do not bring it to me.

The impressive looking lady stood up and offered her hand to Matt as she greeted him. 'Morning, you must be Matt, have a seat,' she said.

'Hello, pleased to meet you,' he replied, as he settled into the small armless leather chair. He watched his new boss as she briefly looked at the clock on the wall and then at him over her narrow spectacles that rested on her nose. Her dark attractive eyes seemed friendly to him.

After a brief look at some papers in front of her, she sat back and put her spectacles on the desk.

'Well Matt; a degree in journalism; with honours,' she said.

'Yes, I was very pleased,' Matt replied.

Diane looked at the clock again. 'Good, well done,' she continued. 'And now I suppose you're eager to get started.'

Matt nodded politely. Diane looked out into the main office and gestured to someone. A few seconds later a tall scruffy man came into the office and said hello as he sat down next to Matt.

'Matt, this is Dave Roundtree, he'll be your mentor until further notice,' said Diane.

She let the two men eye each other up before continuing. 'Look after him, Dave, but not too much. He needs to learn quickly.'

'No worries, boss, he'll be fine with me. Aren't they always?'

'No, not always, remember the last one?' she said.

Dave Roundtree said nothing else as he smiled. Two minutes later Matt was settling down at his own desk next to his new mentor. He decided he would not ask about 'the last one'.

Tuesday 07.40

James Turner, holding his hands out in despair, spoke as calmly as he could as he faced his fellow board members. 'Conflict again. What do I have to do to please these people?'

His operations director, Simon Nunn, stood up to look out of the window. 'There are about 40 workers stood by this gate out here James, on strike. Yesterday it was 30, tomorrow it could be 60. Give them what they're asking for,' he said.

'And what will they give me in return, more productivity?' asked Turner.

Nunn sat down again, shaking his head, without speaking.

Turner turned to the lady on his left. 'What about you, Mary, you're the HR person, what do you say?'

'I say we stick to what we said yesterday.'

'Why?' asked Nunn.

'Because backing down now would set a precedent. They had a three percent increase last year, which is more than most companies in our sector gave.'

Turner turned to the fourth person in the room, finance director Michael Farndon.

'Well, Mike,' he said, 'I agree with Mary, Simon doesn't; what do you say?'

'My answer is factual. We cannot afford it,' said Farndon.

'Right, that's it then,' said Turner.

'And what do I tell those people standing out there?' Nunn asked.

Turner stood to look out of the window toward the main gate. 'Tell them we cannot afford more pay increases,' he said. 'I see the union man is stood with them; he knows where my office is if he wants to talk to me.'

Tuesday 07.43

Matt Melbourne looked up in anticipation as his mentor answered the phone.

'Hello Daily Echo, Dave Roundtree...right...where is this, sir?...okay, and you're sure about this?....not at all, you did right in telling us, many thanks.'

Dave put the phone down, and reached for his mobile and his notebook. He looked into the editor's office to see she was on the telephone looking out on to the street. He smiled and turned to Matt. 'Right, come with me young man, we've got a strike to report.'

Tuesday 08.12

Matt soon realised that Dave Roundtree knew his way around. On the way to the industrial estate Dave had not looked at a map once or tried to consult his sat-nav. The VW Golf was shabby and unkempt, like its owner. As they turned off the main road Dave pointed toward a gathering of people. 'There, that's it, Harold Turner and Son,' he said.

They left the car thirty metres away and walked towards the crowd. A large man with a plaque saying WE NEED MORE confronted them.

'You can't come past here you two, no one can, it's a picket, a strike,' he said.

The experienced reporter told the man what he wanted to hear. 'Absolutely, don't want to, good on yer mate, we all deserve more money, I'm Dave and this is Matt from the Daily Echo, who's in charge then?'

The big man pointed to a man and a woman stood closer to the gate. 'Let them through!' he shouted.

Dave looked at Matt and motioned his head towards the two people. 'Follow me and stay close.'

As they got closer, Dave held up his ID card and had to shout to be heard over the chanting. 'Dave Roundtree, Daily Echo! This is Matt Melbourne!'

'I'm Lucy Dawson, I run the main production line,' the woman said.

The man next to her looked more suspiciously at the two reporters. 'I'm Gary Jones, works steward, manufacturers union, have you got a camera?'

The experienced Dave got down to business quickly. 'Why are you striking?' he said.

'More money, what else?' said the woman.

'This company is way behind the times on pay scales and conditions,' interrupted Jones.

It was then that Dave saw the first chink in the armour. The woman looked quizzically at the works steward. 'They're not that bad, Gary, we just want a bit more pay,' she said.

The crowd became quieter. People were looking towards the main building. James Turner was walking towards them. He had seen Dave and Matt arrive and guessing they were journalists, had decided to make sure they got both sides of the story. As he got closer, the crowd began to shout again and he had to force his way through them to get to Jones and Lucy Dawson. He looked at Dave and Matt and then at the works steward. 'Hope you're not exaggerating again, Gary,' he said.

'I don't exaggerate, Turner, you haven't got a clue, your dad was just the same!'

Dave took out a small camera from his pocket and handed it to Matt. 'Snap away mate, any shots, any angles, go for it.'

Turner moved closer to Dave and grabbed his arm. 'Hope those photos are going to be fair. What paper are you from?'

'Daily Echo, Mr Turner, can we have a quiet word somewhere?'

They forced their way through the crowd until they could stand unhindered. Turner related the story of the last few days as Dave took notes. Suddenly there was a scream and everyone turned to see a clearing appearing in the crowd. The screams had stopped and a young girl was standing with her face in her hands looking down at a man on the floor who was clutching his stomach as blood poured out of it.

'Get an ambulance!' someone shouted.

'What's happened,' said another.

By now Turner had reached the scene. He looked at the man on the floor. It was not anyone he recognised. 'Who is he?' he said.

'Zeckelski, one of those Polish guys that started last week,' someone said.

Two of the protestors, one a first aider, had fetched a first aid kit and some extra bandages. The first aider tried to roll the injured person over, others helped her. Blood was pouring out of his stomach. The hardened Dave Roundtree was quick to act also. He waved to Matt to get pictures of the man on the floor.

Tuesday 08.31

The ambulance arrived and the paramedics went about their business. The injured Polish man had stopped groaning. Turner moved forward again towards them as they both crouched over the man. He put his hand on the shoulder of one of them and spoke quietly. 'What is it, something wrong?'

The younger of the two paramedics looked up and shook his head. 'It doesn't look good, just make plenty of room so we can get him in the ambulance.'

As the ambulance drove away, the crowd subsided and people started to go about their usual business. Turner called for one of his colleagues to get to the hospital. Dave Roundtree pushed some cash into Matt's hand and gave him a clear and precise instruction. 'Get a cab to the Hospital, stay there until you know how the Polish man is.'

Matt nodded quickly and ran towards the main road.

Tuesday 11.50

Diane Mathers came out of her meeting and went straight to Dave Roundtree's desk.

'I take it you got to this strike I heard about?' she said.

'Damn right I did, boss, just writing it up now, did you know about the casualty?'

'No, what's happened? And where's Matt?' she asked.

'Someone got hurt, badly; according to the strikers he was a Polish guy called Zeckelski who joined the firm last week. I sent Matt to the hospital to see how he is; haven't heard anything yet.'

Diane looked concerned and surprised as she replied. 'Bloody hell, Dave, it's his first day here!'

Dave's reply was interrupted by Matt coming through the door.

'Matt, okay mate?' said Dave.

'Yes thanks,' replied Matt.

Diane did not interrupt, she knew what was coming next and would leave it to Dave.

'How is he Matt?' asked Dave.

'He died about thirty minutes ago,' said Matt, 'he'd been stabbed.

Tuesday 12.32

In her office, Diane was checking the story that Dave had written about the strike. Dave was pacing around and turned to her when he could see she had finished. 'What do you think?' he said.

'Good, very good; pictures?' she said.

'Matt's downloading them from the camera now. I'll pick a short list of three or four and let you have a look.'

Diane looked out into the main office to see Matt approaching. 'Looks like he's got them now,' she said.

Matt knocked politely on the door before walking up to both of them. He looked uncomfortable.

'What have we got, Matt?' asked Dave.

'Loads of good shots actually,' replied Matt quietly, 'but er, I had better show you this one first.'

He handed a photo to Dave who raised an eyebrow, hesitated and passed it to Diane. Matt looked at Diane for a response. She hadn't quite noticed what the other two had seen.

'Look at the bottom centre, boss, the small man with red hair,' said Dave.

Diane moved the photo so it got more light from the window and looked closer. The small man was holding a knife with what looked like blood dripping from it.

'So that's the killer,' she said.

'Yes it is,' replied Dave. 'Question is, what do we do now?'

'We print the story without pictures,' she said.

Matt was about to say something when Dave raised his hand and pointed to the door. 'Right, boss, will do. Come on Matt I'll tell you all about going to print.'

Wednesday 07.40

Dave arrived at the office to find Matt already there. He realised he needed to talk to Matt and explain what had happened. 'In case you're wondering, Diane told the police last night and gave them that photo,' he said.

'Okay, thanks. Do we leave it there then?' asked Matt.

'Course we do, the police will have that man by now. The strike is a separate issue and probably all over by now, but it was a good story for your first day eh?'

'Yes I'll say,' said Matt, as he looked at his computer.

Wednesday 12.30

Matt did not feel comfortable. He thought maybe it was too early to be getting reporters hunches but he did have a gut feeling about yesterday's events. How come no one else saw the stabbing, or the knife? How come the police had not been to interview himself or Dave or Diane?

He looked at the clock. Dave had gone out on a minor story and had left him there to file some papers. He looked around to see that another new employee was in the office. She seemed busy on her laptop as he approached her. 'Mind if I pop out for lunch?' he said to her.

'No, you go ahead, I'll be fine,' she said, without looking up.

He drove his car to the place where yesterday's strike had happened and parked on the road, away from the main gate. A few people were coming and going, presumably for lunch, and he settled down to observe and think for a while.

His mobile phone rang. It said *Dave calling.*

'Hello, Dave, I er, I'm just getting a sandwich, sorry, won't be long.'

'Right, quick as you can then, I've got a job for you.'

Matt pulled himself up in his seat and reached for the seatbelt. Then he froze. A man was walking out of the gates of Harold Hunter and Son. He was carrying a hold-all that looked heavy. He was small, with red hair. It was the man in the photograph.

A car with foreign number plates pulled up just outside the gates and the man got in the front passenger seat. Matt thought about the sign on Diane Mathers' office door. He decided to follow the two men in the car.

Wednesday 13.09

Matt parked on the outskirts of the supermarket car park, about one hundred metres away from where the foreign car had parked. The two men did not get out of their car. He phoned Dave Roundtree to explain what had happened and Dave told him to stay where he was until he got there. Twenty five minutes later Dave arrived and parked his scruffy Golf next to Matt's car. He beckoned to Matt to join him.

'How long have they been here?' asked Dave.

'About 35 minutes.'

'Right, we'll wait a while longer and see what happens. Are you okay?'

Matt sighed heavily before answering. 'Not sure.'

Dave patted him on his knee to reassure him. 'You've done well, Matt; I think you'll do okay as a reporter.'

'Thanks, Dave, but why is that man here? If Diane gave the photo to the police they would have got him by now. They obviously didn't even go to the factory because he was there. Why would they not arrest him?'

'I'm not sure Matt, let's see what happens next.'

Wednesday 14.00

A large car pulled alongside the two men in the foreign car.

'So they're meeting someone; who could it be?' said Matt.

'Give me a moment and I'll tell you,' Dave said. He reached for his phone and started to dial. 'Remind me to give you this number one day,' he said to Matt as he waited for his call to be answered.

Matt listened with intrigue as Dave spoke to someone called Frank and read out the number of the large car that had just arrived. The call over, Dave raised an eyebrow and nodded slowly.

'You know who the car belongs to then?' asked Matt.

'Yes; Special Branch.'

Matt was struck dumb. He started to panic. 'But Dave we can't just.....'

'Wait!' interrupted Dave, 'look.'

The hold-all that the small man had carried was being passed to the driver of the large car. The foreign car pulled away and turned to exit the car park. The Special Branch car stayed where it was.

'What now?' asked Matt.

'We stay together, but not with those boys, if they are Special Branch, they'll be on to us pretty soon, we'll follow the foreign car.'

Dave got his Golf moving and followed the foreign car out of the car park. Their trail took them back to the industrial estate. The small man got out of the car and went back into the factory. The driver parked the foreign car near the gate and went into the offices. Dave parked on the road and immediately started to get out of the car as he spoke to Matt. 'Come on mate, I'm striking while the iron's hot.'

Matt followed him. He was scared.

The receptionist, unaware that they had spoken to Turner the day before, greeted them with a smile. Dave gave her his innocent look. 'Hello, I just want to drop something off for a friend; is that okay?' he said.

'No sorry,' she said 'no visitors are allowed past this point.'

'Oh right, well in that case you had better tell Mr Turner that Dave Roundtree wants to see him about yesterdays strike.'

'I'll see if he's free,' said the receptionist, her smile gone now.

Surprisingly, a few minutes later, James Turner entered the reception area. He greeted Dave and Matt and they followed him to his office. Another man was already in the office. It was the driver of the foreign car. He remained seated and looked at Matt and then Dave, but said nothing and Turner did not introduce him to them. Turner turned to the other man as though for approval before addressing Dave and Matt.

'Gents, I need to speak to you about events because it is very important that certain things don't get into your newspaper,' he said.

'Go on, Mr Turner please, we're responsible reporters,' said Dave.

'Do you know what we manufacture here?' asked Turner.

Dave shook his head. Matt stayed silent.

'Detonators,' continued Turner, 'and some of the detonators get to be used in Afghanistan. Army mainly, including the SAS.'

Dave realised that the other man in the room was probably someone important, so he decided to grasp the nettle. He nodded to acknowledge what Turner had said and then looked at the other man.

'Do you mind if I ask who you are sir?' he said.

'My name is Hadleigh, Special Branch,' said the man, who then turned his gaze from Dave to Matt. 'And next time you decide to follow a vehicle young man, you need to keep further back.'

Matt swallowed hard. Dave looked at Hadleigh for more.

'The man you saw with me is one of ours,' said Hadleigh.

'The man who was holding the knife in the photo' replied Dave.

'Yes, the man he killed yesterday worked for a group of Afghan rebels.'

'And what about the bag we saw you hand to the other car in the supermarket car park?' Dave asked, determined to push it as far as he could.

Turner then joined in. 'It contained some modified detonators that the dead man was going to smuggle out of the country.'

Dave pressed on, looking at Hadleigh. 'Can I ask why your colleague is back in the factory then, if you have your man?'

'The dead man was working with someone else in the factory. In the next few moments we should know who. You can have your full story then; and not before.'

There was silence for a few seconds between all four men. Dave thought he knew what was coming so he moved things on. 'What happens now then?' he asked.

'You both stay here with Mr Turner,' said Hadleigh. 'I'm going down to meet my colleague.'

Seconds later Hadleigh was gone and Turner resettled himself in his chair. Dave was making notes and looked up at Matt as he started to pace around the room.

A big sigh from Turner prompted Dave to speak to him. 'Was it your father who started the business Mr Turner? I noticed the name, Harold Turner and Son.'

'Yes it was. Before all this kicked off, I was ready to retire and sell the business. Then Hadleigh came to see me. I decided to see this out first.'

'And the other person working with the dead man sir? Any ideas who it is?'

'No, absolutely none; and Hadleigh has said nothing. But in the next few minutes we should know; he said they were going to arrest someone this afternoon.'

Wednesday 15.04

As Matt paced around the room he was intrigued how he could feel such fright and excitement at the same time. He looked briefly out the office window to see two police cars pull up and block the main gates to the factory. Turner and Dave, still seated, did not notice the cars and for a reason that Matt could not explain to himself, he did not tell them. Then he realised he still had the camera in his pocket. He turned to Turner as casually as he could. 'Are the toilets nearby?' he asked.

'Turn left out of the door, second on your right,' said Turner.

Dave looked up. 'Be quick, Matt, okay? And straight back here.'

'Right.' Matt replied.

Matt did visit the toilets. But he did not go back to the office.

He moved quickly down the stairs and past the receptionist. She looked at him with indifference, obviously unaware of what was happening, he thought. He made his way towards the production line where he had seen Hadleigh go when he was looking out of the window. Checking the camera was ready for use, he stood by the door that led to the production line.

At that moment, he thought about the receptionist. Why had she not challenged him? Earlier she had told him and Dave that no one was allowed past reception to this area.

Then the door he was standing next to was thrown open. The first man to appear was the small red-headed man carrying another hold-all. Then a woman appeared. She was handcuffed to Hadleigh. She hesitated for a while as she looked at Matt. It was Lucy Dawson, the woman that Dave had spoken to at the strike yesterday. Hadleigh shoved her from behind and shouted. 'Move Dawson! Just keep walking.'

Matt felt the arm grab him round the neck. Someone had come up from behind. He nearly stumbled as his attacker pulled him back and forced the barrel of a gun into the side of his neck. He tried to fight back but the attacker was too experienced and kept him off balance. As he turned slightly in the struggle he could see a reflection in an office window. His attacker was the receptionist.

By now the other three had almost reached one of the police cars. The receptionist pulled Matt away from the building and faced him toward them. 'Stop now!' she yelled.

Hadleigh, Dawson and the red haired man turned quickly to see what was happening.

The receptionist shouted again. 'Let her go! Take off the cuffs and let her go! I will kill this boy if you do not!'

'And then what about you?' Hadleigh shouted back.

'The boy will come with me! If you follow I will kill him!'

Hadleigh only thought for a while. He knew she would kill him anyway. He nodded his head slightly to make the signal. The crack of the rifle, the receptionist being thrown back as the bullet hit her in the head and Matt being covered in her blood all happened in less than a second.

Thursday 07.35

'Well Matt, how are you today?' asked Diane.

'Not too bad thank you.'

'I've told him off about yesterday, boss,' said Dave. 'I think he'll do as he's told next time.'

'Right, well let's get it written up then,' said Diane. 'Have you got all the details?'

'Yes, we.....'

'Yes we have,' interrupted Matt. 'Lucy Dawson and the receptionist both worked for an Afghan rebel group, so did the dead man, I've got pictures too.'

Diane looked at Matt and spoke to him sternly. 'Good, but next time do as you're told and don't interrupt your mentor like that.'

'Yes, boss,' said Matt quietly.

Diane turned to Dave with a faint smile and then looked at Matt again. 'Right then, heed what you have been told young man.'

Matt moved sheepishly back to his desk and looked up as Diane spoke again. 'Oh, and er, Matt; well done.'

A Cat's Tale.

Domestic life through the eyes of a cat

Both of them were arguing as usual. He was going on about the cost of electricity and she was telling him she didn't really care.

He had arrived home from work at the usual time and poured himself a beer, before going through the mail. It was obviously an electricity bill or something similar that had started it all off. She had been cooking something again in that big pot thing; I could smell the meat.

After a while, and a change of clothes for him, they settled down to eat. I made my way to the sofa in my usual nonchalant way to settle down and wait for them. They wouldn't be long; Holby City was on soon.

As I waited, I started to think back to when I was young and how I had ended up being here. I recalled how, as a kitten, I would play with my mum in the house where I had been born. My brother, a daft looking black and white thing with an attitude problem, would normally get jealous and join in and my mum would play with him as well; much to my annoyance. Luckily, I had inherited my father's beautiful shiny black coat and good looks, so I always had that to fall back on for the 'ah' factor.

A few months later when the Family From Hell came to collect me, I was devastated. The main reason for this was that they changed my name; to Sheila! Now, I am not miserable, I take things as they come and get on with it. But I am a male. How no person ever realised this I will never know. Anyway, Family From Hell had money problems I gathered and I ended up in a cattery.

The people who ran the cattery were okay, but not brilliant. I got the feeling that they could have tried harder to find me a home. So when these two collected me a year ago, I was quite pleased. But I do remember one of the cattery girls saying something like 'he wasn't best pleased having to stump up five hundred quid'. Excuse me, I thought, I am a pedigree! Well at least they gave me a proper name; Louis. Apparently because I was black and I groaned like Louis Armstrong, whoever he is.

Anyway; on this particular night they both joined me as per usual; one either side. She was stroking me too much and when I tried to tell her with a succinct little miaow, he would call me a miserable git. You humans can be a little testy sometimes.

Holby had been on for about half an hour when the phone rang. She answered it; she always did, it was rarely for him. The look on her face told me there was a problem. He touched that little square thing and the television went quiet.

'Yes we're both in now,' she said. After a while she spoke again. 'Yes I suppose so. Okay then.'

'Who was that?' he asked.

'The RSPCA; that inspector that we spoke to last year when Libby went missing. Someone found a cat this afternoon that looks like her. He wants to bring it round so we can have a look at it.'

A cold shiver went down my back. Who the flipping heck was Libby? My predecessor perhaps?

The television noise came on again and he finished his beer. 'It can't be Libby,' he said. 'It's been over a year.'

'You never know, cats go missing for ages and find their way back,' she said.

I decided to stay where I was and not show concern. She came back to the sofa and started stroking me again. She spoke to me in that awful girlish voice she puts on when she is adoring me. It can be so embarrassing. 'Well Louis, my beautiful boy, we may be getting our Libby back. You will like her Louis, I know you will.'

Wrong.

'Let's just wait first, and see,' he said in his authoritative voice.

Yes, well said, I thought. But hang on; I need a plan don't I, just in case? What though? I looked at both of them. She was nervous and had stopped stroking me. Yee gods! She's stopped thinking about me already!

He answered the door about 30 minutes later. She turned the television off. The RSPCA man looked nice enough. He was smiling gently as they ushered him in and offered him a seat. He was carrying a cat box. He was carrying a cat box! They sat down either side of me again and the RSPCA man turned the box round so the mesh door was facing the two of them. And there it was! A female, about five years old, white, with a few dark stripes down her sides. I pretended to remain aloof.

'Okay if I let her out?' asked the man.

'Oh yes of course,' she said, as she sat forward away from me in anticipation. He sat back and said nothing. When the door opened, it walked out slowly. Then it stood still and looked at me; then at the other two. A few seconds later, it let out a pathetic little miaow and came walking towards her. They definitely knew each other. Oh flipping heck! I decided to make my mark. As it got closer to the sofa, I let out one of my scary growls. It froze. I stared at it.

'Oh shut up, Louis,' she said.

'I don't believe it, this *is* Libby,' he said.

The RSPCA man asked him if he was sure. He nodded and she confirmed it. 'Oh we're sure, I can't believe it.'

The cat, still looking at me, walked up to her and rubbed itself against her legs. She picked it up and kissed its head. I got off the sofa in disgust and walked over to the other side of the room to position myself strategically.

'Will you be keeping both of them now then?' asked the RSPCA man.

'Of course we will! This is marvelous isn't it darling!' she said.

'Yes I guess so,' he said with reservation.

They signed a couple of forms and the RSPCA man left. He said he couldn't wait for too long; something about a bird trapped in a chimney.

She carried the cat out into the kitchen. 'Come on Libby, I'll show you where the cat dish is. You can share it with Louis.'

What! I looked at him and gave him a long moody miaow.

He looked down at me and shrugged his shoulders. 'Don't look at me, mate, she's back with us and that's it.'

After a few hours of trite remarks, both of them went to bed. The cat followed them up the stairs. I waited for a while before making my move. This was a job for Big Ed down the road.

I made my way quietly out the cat flap and headed towards number 36. As usual Big Ed was lying outside his front door looking majestic. I gave him the 'need your help' growl and he followed me back. We made our way stealthily up the stairs towards the bedroom. I stopped and

38

gave Big Ed the nod to go ahead of me. It was as he was passing me that I was reminded of just how big he was, his ginger stripes glowing in the dark.

Trouble is, Libby wasn't in that room. She was behind us!

Her claw caught me right on the bum, I spun round and lashed out, but she was too quick for me, she was already doing about 50 miles an hour down the stairs. Big Ed had heard it and he came rushing past me in pursuit, I followed him down. As I got to the dining room I spotted Libby. She was sitting on the edge of table looking down at Big Ed with an air of cheekiness as if to say, come on then fat boy, just try it. Big Ed was looking up at her, growling. After a while, Libby assumed the prone position, her stare not leaving him. He turned around and looked at me, shrugged his shoulders and left.

Well, Big Ed wasn't getting any younger.

The following morning, I was first up as usual. Those two were still in bed when I made my way downstairs. Normally I would have bothered them both and wrapped myself around her head to purr, which always got me a few brownie points, but I knew Libby had stayed downstairs all night and I wanted to see what she had been up to. That's a shame, I thought as I looked around; no breakages, no food on the floor, everything looking neat and tidy. I was hoping to see some damage so Libby would be blamed for it. I took up my morning position on the sofa.

CRASH! What was that? I sprinted outside to where the noise had come from. Libby was standing on the patio covered in soil, the old man's best flower pot in smithereens around her. She had knocked it off his bench. After a brief pause, she ran into a corner of the garden to hide. Big Ed had heard the noise and he was coming round the corner just as the old man reached the scene of the crime in his pyjamas. 'Get out of here!' he shouted to Big Ed, who turned and coolly wandered off. I miaowed as loudly as I could; it wasn't Big Ed you fool! It was *her*.

And to this day, she never gets the blame. She can't do anything wrong! Mind you, the quality of the food has improved, (They don't know I eat most of it) I got a new bed and there are more toys to kick about. I think Libby is warming to me and that she realises who is in charge. I am, of course, and I say that with confidence.

I think.

Deadly games

An unfaithful husband gets a shock

Caroline Fletcher let her handbag slide off her shoulder onto the armchair. She kicked off her shoes, poured out the usual large glass of Chardonnay with ice and switched on the television. Benny the cat had his usual look of indifference as he came to sit next to her. She checked her mobile phone for any messages, as she always did when her husband was away on business. She reached for the remote and clicked on the television. The first news item was about money, the second about a stabbing. She switched it off again and stroked Benny. 'Same old stuff, eh boy?'

Craig Fletcher arrived at his hotel in Oxford a little later than usual that evening. He had become accustomed to his three nights away each week and as usual would phone Caroline when he was settled in the bar with a glass of wine.

Putting his newspaper to one side, he pressed short dial one. Caroline was quick to answer and he could tell by the tone of her voice that there was a story coming.

'Be careful down there won't you if you go out tonight' she said jokingly.

'Why, what's happened?' he asked.

'Oh just joking, something on the news about knife crime again tonight. Had a good day?'

'Mm, not too bad, you?'

'Usual really, Dorothy in the accounts department has had another warning; I think if it happens again, Charles will just sack her.'

'Right, if you're okay then I'll phone you again tomorrow,' said Craig, seeming uninterested.

'All right then, take care,' she said.

'All right, you too; bye.'

As Caroline put the phone down, a feeling of sadness came over her. His calls were getting shorter and shorter; almost as though he was only phoning her out of a sense of duty rather than want.

The following afternoon Craig finished a little earlier. His mind was not as it should have been. During the day's meetings, his thoughts had wandered and he knew that once again that night, he would be unfaithful to his wife.

He was sure that he still loved and wanted her, but after just four years of marriage, their relationship had taken a back seat to their careers. Caroline had just been made a full partner at the surgery where she worked and she was determined to show her fellow male GPs what she was made of. Craig, the all too common, thirty something workaholic, had been and always would be, very ambitious.

As Craig left the hotel that night, the duty manager greeted him.

'Mr Fletcher, how are you, sir?'

'Yes, fine thanks, and you?'

44

'Yes thank you, sir. Not dining with us tonight?'

'Not tonight, meeting a friend for a Chinese, tomorrow maybe.'

'Okay, sir, have a good evening.'

As Craig pulled into the car park of the Chinese restaurant, he could see his 'friend' waiting for him. He had only seen her twice before and she infatuated him. They had first met in a pub near where he worked. She had bumped into him as he turned from the bar with drinks in hand. After swapping a few text messages that afternoon, they met in the evening at her flat. She had been insatiable and they had made love for hours. The second time they met, he had taken her back to his hotel and same thoughts were in his mind again.

She opened his door for him as he came to a stop. As he got from the car she grasped her hands around his buttocks and kissed him. Her perfume intoxicated him once again as he kissed her nape. 'I've put your favourite, Rive Gauche, on for you,' she said.

As they dined, Craig could tell that she was feeling insatiable again. Her high heels constantly stroked his legs and he could feel his already high libido was starting to want her. She finished her wine and put her hand on his wrist. 'Shall we go then? Your hotel or my place?'

Craig smiled as he thought of the last time they were at the hotel. 'My hotel, but you really do need to tell me your name. I can't keep saying you're a business colleague. You're too sexy to be a business colleague.'

'Okay, tell them I'm your wife.'

'I can't, she has stays with me sometimes remember. The hotel staff know her.'

'Oh just tell them what you like, none of their business anyway.'

45

Craig was somewhat surprised at her tone as she spoke. It was a hard tone he had not heard before. He decided to push the point. She wanted him, he thought, more than he wanted her. 'No come on, what is your name?'

'Oh alright, if it matters to you, Dawn.'

'Dawn what?'

'Oh what does it matter, come on let's get back so I can get your kit off!'

'Dawn what?'

'Dawn Thomas. Alright?'

'Okay, Dawn Thomas, let's go.'

On the way back to the hotel she spoke to him as her hand was caressing his thigh. 'Anyway I don't know your last name, I only know the Craig bit.'

'It's Fletcher, Craig Fletcher at your service madam.'

Caroline Fletcher had made good time. The road from Bristol to Oxford was quiet for early evening. Her husband was always away and the loneliness at home was becoming all too familiar and predictable. On the odd occasion, she had accompanied him when he stayed away, but his heavy workload had always somehow come first and their evenings had not been exciting. This time, she had decided, it was going to be different.

She knew from Craig's telephone calls and texts that he had dinner in the hotel about seven, followed by a drink in the bar before returning to his room to watch the television or read a book.

She had planned everything to the last detail. Craig did not know she was off work that day. The sexiest underwear she owned still looked good on her and the high heels were Craig's favourite. It was a cold day and her overcoat kept her warm as she drove, which was just as well as she was not wearing a dress underneath it.

As she got closer to the hotel she began to get excited. Poor Craig, she thought, always sounds fed up when I speak to him. She felt naughty, like a high class call girl, but their marriage needed a few things like this and she loved him so much.

As Craig and Dawn arrived back at the hotel, no one was in reception. Craig held her hand and they quickly ran down the corridor to his room like two mischievous school children. The room was warm and quiet. Dawn turned the television on.

'Why do you want that on?' said Craig.

Dawn took his tie off and started to undo his trousers. 'To drown the noise of my screams,' she said.

'Mm, you're one hell of a woman' he replied as he lifted her slightly and pushed her back onto the bed.

KNOCK, KNOCK, KNOCK

Dawn, startled, sat up. Craig held his finger to his mouth and sounded a quiet 'sh.' He looked quizzical and shrugged his shoulders as he looked at Dawn and then turned his head toward the door.

'Hello?' he said.

A foreign sounding voice replied, 'room service.'

He looked at Dawn and whispered, 'I haven't ordered room service.'

'Oh let them in anyway,' she whispered 'we'll be hungry later.'

'Right, get in the bathroom and shut the door, they'll know you're not my wife.'

Dawn gathered her clothes and shuffled into the bathroom. Craig adjusted his attire and opened the door.

Caroline moved forward to be in the doorway. 'Like I said, Mr Fletcher, room service.'

She unbuttoned her coat slowly and held it open so Craig could clearly see what she was wearing. Craig swallowed hard and took a deep breath. 'Right, err, okay. Wow.'

He moved to one side so Caroline could walk in. As she did, she turned, dropped her coat to the floor and kissed him. Craig was lost for words, he knew he must not resist because she would get suspicious. After a few moments he pulled away from her and made a suggestion. 'Look no rush, we should enjoy this, let's go down to the bar and have some champagne.'

'Why not have it in the room?' asked Caroline.

'Because I need to pay for it at the bar, the company checks invoices now and again remember.'

'Oh yes; I'll just put my coat back on and while we're downstairs it will be our secret my darling.'

Craig smiled and led her to the door. She smirked as she passed him in the doorway and walked down the corridor like a woman on a catwalk as Craig followed her.

An hour later as they were finishing the champagne, Caroline reminded him of how she was feeling as she crossed her legs and deliberately let her coat come apart around her knees. Craig looked at her and raised his eyebrows. Surely, he thought, Dawn would be gone by now. He leaned over and kissed Caroline. 'Coffee?'

Caroline looked bemused and she was surprised even further when he picked up a nearby newspaper.

'You're not serious,' she said.

'What.'

'What? For god's sake, Craig!'

'Okay, Okay, keep your voice down.'

'Sod my voice. I go to all this trouble to please you and you pick up a blasted newspaper!'

Some of the hotel bar clientele looked around at the raised voices. Craig put the paper down and held out his down turned hands in a calming gesture. 'Alright, alright, don't get loud, people are looking.'

Caroline turned her head away and sighed. Craig looked at her. I've got this wrong, he thought to himself. What do I say now? He decided to take the lead. 'Well, that's spoilt the whole thing then now hasn't it,' he said. 'Come on then, let's go back to the room.'

He led the way back upstairs and took a deep breath as he opened the door. Caroline, still upset sat on the bed without speaking.

'I need the bathroom, won't be long,' Craig said. He opened the bathroom door praying the place would be empty. It was.

He took a deep breath and went to turn on the cold water. He stood back for while, shocked. The huge wall mirror behind the basin was shattered. Glass was all over the surfaces and in the basin. A single blow to the middle of the mirror had splintered it outwards like an exploded star. The left hand section of the mirror was still intact, and on it were written the words, YOU LOVE ME - NOT HER - YOU BASTARD.

He grabbed the nearest towel and started to rub frantically. Luckily, whatever it was came off without too much trouble, probably a cheap lipstick or something like that, he thought.

Caroline walked into the bathroom. 'Oh my god, what is it!'

'Heaven knows,' Craig replied 'someone must have been in while we were downstairs. I'll go and see the duty manager, you stay here.'

The duty manager was sympathetic to Craig's story; he had slipped and hit his head on the mirror as he was getting out of the bath. He would of course pay for it.

Back in the room, Caroline was getting undressed. For the rest of the night, they lay next to each other not talking or touching. At 3 a.m. Craig, still awake, looked at Caroline as she slept. His mind was in turmoil. Why? He thought to himself. You're an idiot, Craig Fletcher, an idiot.

The following morning they drove back to Bristol in convoy. Caroline was constantly checking in her rear view mirror to see how Craig was looking. When they had to stop a couple of times and he came up right behind her, he could not look at her eyes in her mirror and turned his head to one side. She knew then that perhaps their marriage was over.

The house was cold when they arrived at 11 a.m. In an effort to act normally, Craig put the kettle on and offered coffee. They sat down in the lounge and talked for a while about what had happened. Craig could sense all was not right with Caroline. He put his arm around her. 'Bit of an idiot sometimes aren't I? Sorry.'

Caroline moved away and sat on another chair. After a few seconds she answered him. 'Yes, you are. And I'm not sure I can endure it.'

Craig did not answer. He started to feel indifferent about it all. Caroline was not looking at him. He was thinking of another woman and how she would want him if Caroline didn't.

'Right well let's just forget about it for now,' he said. 'I'm going to unpack.'

'Do what you like,' said Caroline.

That evening they did eat together at the table, but the conversation had a staleness to it. Caroline knew something was wrong and she guessed it was another woman. She thought about all of the nights he had spent away in Oxford and how often he had sounded uninterested when she had phoned him. She left him to clear up the dishes and sat down to see what was on the television. She did not really want to watch it but what was the point in talking anymore, she thought.

As she sat back the TV was coming to life, and the newsreader was mentioning some breaking news.

'...so we are going to stay with the subject of knife crime, following our report yesterday that a man was stabbed to death in a frenzied knife attack. It's believed a woman is...'

Caroline turned to another channel, just as Craig was walking from the kitchen. 'Can you just turn it back again,' he said. 'What was that about knife crime?' He had heard what the newsreader had said and the broken mirror back at the hotel had come to his mind. Caroline turned back to the news.

'.....Thames Valley police have just confirmed that they have arrested and charged a woman for the recent knife attacks in Oxford. She has been named as 35 year old Dawn Thomas, who preyed on guests in hotels near where she lived and....'

The plates Craig Fletcher was holding, smashed as they hit the floor.

For Queen and Country

A man's work comes too close to home

Alison Carter knew her husband's life was at risk.

She had actually become accustomed to the reality of it. They had met ten years earlier in a small police station in Cumbria. Alison was working as an admin assistant and her soon to be husband, Roger, had been sent to Cumbria to help the local CID in a *sting* operation against some money launderers. Roger Carter had worked his way up through the ranks and was a senior MI5 agent, specialising in drugs and people trafficking.

Now, ten years on, they were both in their mid forties and enjoying life together in London. Roger was still working for MI5 and Alison helped out at the local hospital in between walking the dogs – Bonnie and Jasper - and visiting her frail mother-in-law nearby.

As she sat in front of her dressing table mirror, Alison thought of the phone call she had received earlier that morning, at about seven, just after Roger had left to catch a flight to Portugal 'on business'. After failing to get in touch with him, she had text him in the hope he would pick up the message as soon as he landed. The phone call had shocked her.

'Mrs Carter?' the foreign sounding voice had said.

'Yes. Who's speaking?'

'Mrs Carter you don't need to know who I am, you just need to listen to what I am about to tell you.'

At this point Alison hit the 'record' button and the Blue button as she had been trained to, which immediately sent a signal to MI5 communications.

'Go on.' She said.

'Your husband, Roger; he needs to retire Mrs Carter. He has been in this game too long. He could be in danger of being seriously hurt Mrs Carter. I wonder; perhaps you could persuade him to retire. It would be beneficial to both of you.'

'Well if you tell me who you are, it might make it a bit easier for me, so I could tell him who is concerned for him.'

'Very good Mrs Carter, or may I call you Alison?'

Alison did not answer. The caller continued. 'You are good Alison. You have obviously had the usual next of kin training. However, let me continue. Your husband needs to retire or we will retire him. Do you understand?'

'Yes I understand.'

'Good, oh and err Alison, I hope your two dogs stay healthy also. They look like nice dogs.'

The plane landed at Lisbon on time. Roger Carter was to meet the local representative of Interpol. He switched his mobile phone on to find the message from Alison. After phoning her to see if she was alright, he got in touch with the London office who redirected the recorded phone call his wife had received to his mobile. As he waited for his transport he received another text message on his phone. – *Hope you got the message Mr Carter. You really should retire.*

His contact from Interpol soon appeared and they made their way to the Lisbon office. A return flight had already been booked for the following morning. The Portuguese section of Interpol had been dealing with a drugs trafficking case that involved export to the UK. The local section commander explained the problem. 'We think it's Raymond Chereau, Mr Carter, the French underworld crime man, and you know how nasty they can be.'

'Indeed, commander, I do. They want me to 'retire'.

The commander handed some documents over to Carter. 'In here is every bit of information and evidence your people should need to apprehend these people. We expect them to land in England in two days, by sea.'

Alison looked at the clock in her kitchen. It was 6 p.m. Hopefully Roger would be back with her in about 12 to 14 hours. Meanwhile, Larry Heddon was with her, sitting in the lounge drinking his lemonade. She had known Larry for quite a while. He was a good friend of her and Roger and was often looked upon as Roger's protégé in MI5. He was good, but had quite a way to go before he could match his mentor.

An hour later as they both sat in the kitchen, there was the sound of the front door letterbox being opened. Heddon pointed towards a corner of the room. Alison moved there quickly. After waiting for two minutes Heddon moved towards the front porch and opened the inner door slowly. The front door was still locked shut. An envelope was hanging from the letterbox. He removed it slowly and retreated into the lounge.

'Okay Alison, come out. It's alright. You have a delivery.'

Alison opened the letter. Inside it were two photographs of her and the two dogs walking in the nearby park that she used.

'Jesus Larry they've been following me!'

'Right, I'll let the squad know. These people are trying to scare you into action.'

'What action?'

'To get you to persuade Roger to retire. Where are the dogs by the way?'

'Upstairs lying on the bed feeling miserable, like they always are when Roger's away.'

Heddon smiled and sat down again. 'Well pointless trying to see who it was. They'll be long gone by now.'

Roger tried to get an earlier flight home but the 6 a.m. the following day was the earliest. He started to look through the dossier that Interpol had given him. There was certainly some important information in there and he began to realise why the perpetrators wanted him out of the picture. By now, they probably knew that he had the information.

Back in London, Alison had almost fallen asleep. It was 2 a.m. She came out of her doze with a nervous jump as there was a knock on the front door. Heddon moved towards the door and looked at her reassuringly. 'It's alright; I'm expecting another of our boys about now to take over from me. Bill Lynton? you've probably met him at one of the Christmas gatherings.'

'Yes, the name rings a bell.' Alison replied.

Heddon went to the front door and stood to one side of it. 'Bill, that you?'

'Yeah, course it is.' Came the reply from the other side.

Heddon unlocked the door and opened it a few inches. The bullet hit him in the stomach. As he went down a large boot kicked him in the face and knocked him back, the second bullet went into his neck. Alison screamed,

'Larry! God Larry! Aah! No, no, no!' She moved into the corner of the room. The two dogs ran down the stairs. Bonnie went straight to her and Alison held her close to her body. Jasper stood in the doorway, his back up and his head down, but he stayed in the doorway. Two men entered the room slowly. One was small and thin, a gun in his hand. The other was tall, more than six feet, with a cruel face that did not suit his smart clothes. The small one spoke first. 'Hello, Mrs Carter, it's nice to speak to you again.' Alison recognised the voice from the telephone call.

The tall man sat down without saying anything. He looked around the room and beckoned to Jasper. 'Come on boy, come here boy.' Jasper ignored him and retreated a few feet back before lying down where he could see everything. The small man spoke to Alison. 'Please Mrs Carter, sit next to me.'

Alison did not move or talk. The small man spoke again and patted the space on the sofa next to him. 'Please Mrs Carter, I insist.'

As she sat next to him she could smell the lingering burning fumes coming from his gun that he had rested on his lap. She sat dead still. He put his hand on her shoulder. She was shaking, the sweat dripping from her face. He moved his hand down her back and put his leg against hers. 'You should have told me you were attractive, Alison, I may have been kinder to you when we spoke. Just relax, I'm really not that bad.'

The tall man was smiling, looking at his colleague. He moved to a chair that was closer to them and challenged his colleague. 'Well, you probably have a few hours, why don't you show her how we appreciate attractive women?'

The small man looked at Alison's breasts. 'Well, Mrs Carter, I mean Alison, why don't I?

Alison said nothing. She was close to feinting.

The mood changed suddenly as the small man got to his feet. 'Right Aldo, get rid of the body out there. I'll let the boss know we're in.'

Both of them went into action. Heddon's body was dragged into the back yard. Bonnie tried to get in the way and the tall man kicked her hard, sending her reeling against the door. She moved away and curled up in the corner. The small man took out his mobile phone and pressed one button. 'It's Angelo, boss, we're in. Any news from Mr Carter?...okay then...will do.' He threw his phone down on a chair and looked at Alison. 'It seems your husband has not responded to our request for him to retire. He's still on his way to London with something that we need.'

Alison tried not to feint. She knew she must say nothing and not look at them.

'This could be interesting, Aldo,' the small man said to his colleague 'the boss is on way to London as well.'

Their boss was Raymond Chereau, the French underworld crime man that Interpol had told Roger Carter about. There was big money at stake and other people's lives didn't really matter to this man and his mobsters.

Roger's plane landed on time at Gatwick a few hours later. His chief of staff at MI5, Commander Stone, was there to meet him.

'What the hell has happened Commander? You wouldn't be here if nothing had happened.'

'Come on, Roger, I'll tell you on the way.'

The car passed through the secluded perimeter gate and made its way up the M23 at great speed. Commander Stone was aware that only the truth must be told in such serious circumstances. 'It looks like two of Chereau's men have got Alison, Roger, in the house. We found Bill Lynton's body just down the road from there and there's been no word from Larry either. Word is that they want to see us destroy that dossier you're carrying or they'll kill her.'

Roger was shocked, but not enough to dull his thoughts. 'So what the hell were Lynton and Heddon playing at, bloody amateurs!'

'I'm sure they did their best, Roger.'

'Yes well it wasn't bloody good enough was it!'

The driver of the car put his foot down even harder. They would be at the house in 30 minutes.

Raymond Chereau's driver was also on his way to the house. Chereau was sitting beside him. He gave his instruction. 'When we get there I'll wait in the car. You go in and tell Aldo to bring the woman out.'

The driver Nodded as he concentrated on the road. 'We'll be there in about 30 minutes, boss.'

Commander Stone was also giving his instructions to his driver. 'Pull up about 50 metres from the house. Roger and I will check it out on foot.

As the driver approached he pulled into a parking space and turned his engine off.

Roger spoke first. 'Stay here, Commander. I'll go in.'

'Oh no you don't, this is too...'

'Stay here, Commander, no offence, but you're past it. Wait for the backup. They're on their way I take it?'

Neither of them had time to discuss it any longer. Another car was pulling up slowly behind them. A man got out and walked toward the house. Roger moved quickly. He jumped from the car, emptied his shoulder holster, and shouted, 'You, stop!'

The man turned, Roger shot him. He went down. Chereau was now also out of the car, shotgun in hand. The first blast took out the back window of Commander Stone's car, but he was falling to the floor before he had chance to let off the second shot. Commander Stone and Roger looked at each other. Neither had shot him. Then four armed policemen appeared from nowhere. Back up had got there early.

Inside the house Alison's captures had heard the shots. So had Alison, and it reminded her of something. Roger always had a gun taped to the underside of the coffee table, just in case.

The cruel faced tall man turned to his colleague. 'Something's gone wrong.'

'I know, Aldo, 'said the small man as he looked at Alison. 'You know what to do.'

Alison knew she had to act now. She cried loudly and fell to the floor so she could get closer to the coffee table. Then she noticed Jasper had inched forward and was now in the room. She cried again. 'No, no please, no... Jasper go!'

The dog was quick. In less than 2 seconds he was on the tall man. His jaw firmly around his wrist. He bit hard. Blood gushed from the man's wrist. The man shouted to his accomplice. 'Kill them! Kill them both now!'

As both men's eyes were on Jasper, Alison reached under the coffee table, ripped the gun off, cocked it and fired twice. The small man was knocked back onto the floor. The tall man, still trying to fight off jasper, looked at her, hatred in his eyes. She looked at him, stood motionless for a while and then pulled the trigger. Jasper let go of his wrist as he fell to the floor. Alison collapsed on the floor, weeping. Jasper and Bonnie both came to her side.

The front door was flung open. Two armed men rushed in followed by Roger and Commander Stone.

They looked at the two men, one dead, the other dying, and then at Alison. Roger rushed over to her and held her.

'You're too late,' she said looking at both of them 'You're too late, I've done your dirty sticking work for you!'

An hour later Commander Stone was holding Roger's arm as he stood by his car. 'When they've cleaned it all up Roger, take Alison away somewhere for a few days, take as long as you need.'

Roger shook his head. 'That won't be necessary Commander. I quit. As of now.'

'Roger come on, the spur of the moment and all that, you need to rest. You know you love this job, you know how much we need you and how much your Queen and Country need you. Come on old boy.'

'Look, Commander, I've been caring for my Queen and Country for nearly twenty years. It's over. I'm now going to spend the rest of my life caring for my wife. Goodbye.'

The Commander looked at him and at Alison who he could see over Roger's shoulder in the doorway. She was kneeling with Jasper at her side. 'Goodbye, Roger. Good luck.'

Have you read?

Ruthless

Stephen W Follows

When a special agent from the Canadian Secret Service is shot dead in Munich, Tom Delaney is given the task of finding out why. When Delaney and his team are attacked by rocket fire, it soon becomes clear that their adversaries mean business - because $90 million is at stake and crime boss, Alan Farrah, will kill anyone for that sort of money without batting an eyelid.

And anyone's life could be in jeopardy when Farrah employs the highest paid hit man in Europe; A cruel heartless man who works from his wheelchair.

A ferocious manhunt through Europe results in death and suffering for the hunter and the hunted. The ruthless men responsible for the crimes are finally cornered as Delaney discovers that the informant is a high-ranking government official - very high.

But it doesn't end there. Waiting patiently in the background is another agent; a woman who has made a promise to avenge her lover.

Out now ISBN 978-0-9566 109-0-4

Stephenwfollows.co.uk